T0195960

A Nasty Virus has Struck the World,

so the Giraffes Stay Home to Stay Safe

Written by: Julie Sorenson

Illustrated by: Richelle Bower

Archway Publishing books may be ordered through booksellers or by contacting:

Archway Publishing
1663 Liberty Drive
Bloomington, IN 47403
www.archwaypublishing.com
1 (888) 242-5904

Because of the dynamic nature of the Internet, any web addresses or links contained in this book may have changed since publication and may no longer be valid. The views expressed in this work are solely those of the author and do not necessarily reflect the views of the publisher, and the publisher hereby disclaims any responsibility for them.

Any people depicted in stock imagery provided by Getty Images are models, and such images are being used for illustrative purposes only.
Certain stock imagery © Getty Images.

Interior Image Credit: Richelle Bower

ISBN: 978-1-4808-9275-0 (sc)
ISBN: 978-1-4808-9276-7 (e)

Print information available on the last page.

Archway Publishing rev. date: 08/19/2020

Author Dedication

I dedicate this book to my family. I am so grateful for your support and encouragement in anything that I do. I appreciate your patience, love, and guidance but mostly your encouragement. Thank you to my husband and my children for pushing me to be the best that I can be, even when I question if I can do it.

I love you with my entire heart and am so thankful to have you by my side as I test the waters with my whimsical, carefree side. You are the biggest supporters and why I continue to push myself to do more.

I also want to thank my mom for believing that I can do anything that I put my mind to. My dad, if he were still alive, he would be so proud that I published a book.

Finally, I want to thank all my students past, present and future for teaching me something every day and for making me want to be the best that I can be for all of you.

Illustrator Dedication

RB. This book is dedicated to my students, past and present, and future. "Fill all your spaces with color."

Samantha Gene and Jersey Jack are two giraffes that have had to stay home for the last few weeks.

They don't understand why they can't go to school, to the park, to the grocery store, or have play dates with their friends. The giraffes are starting to become worried.

Samantha Gene, the younger of the two giraffes, said to Jersey Jack

"Something is not right. I don't know what's going on, things seem stressful in our family right now. I wish we could go about our normal day with our normal routines. Nothing is normal and I feel scared."

Jersey Jack was older and thought that he knew a little bit about what was going on from overhearing the news and talking to his friends on social media. He wasn't supposed to be on social media, so he did not talk to his family about what he had heard. He didn't want to get in trouble for using social media or eavesdropping when his parents were watching the news. He definitely didn't want to worry Samantha Gene.

The next few days Samantha Gene and Jersey Jack ramped up their behaviors. Samantha Gene would cry a lot and throw things. She reverted back to some of her younger outgrown behaviors like cuddling extra, using her blanket, and sucking her hoof.

Jersey Jack, on the other hand, started talking back and arguing with his sister. He was sleeping more, noncompliant, and downright rude.

Finally, Georgia, the giraffe's mom, said to Jose, their stepdad, "We need to talk to the kids. It seems like they are showing us that they are stressed by the outbursts they are having. I am sure they notice that their schedule and routines are off."

Jose responded, "Okay, but we need to reassure them that this is an adult-size problem. Their job is to be kids and to know that they can always talk to us, we are here for them."

Georgia called a family meeting. They all met around the dining room table. Georgia was the first one to speak. The kids knew it was not good if a meeting was called. They were extra nervous with big, bright, scared eyes. "Kids, I have noticed a change in your attitudes and I am sure that you notice things are a little off right now. We wanted to see what you know, what questions you have, and how we can help you."

Jose chimed in, "You can tell us anything. We are here for you and we want to help you through this."

Samantha Gene spoke first, "I want to go to school and grandma and grandpa's house. I haven't seen my best friend Paige, in four weeks. You won't take us to the grocery store. Jersey isn't going to baseball practice and neither one of you is going to work."

Jersey Jack started raising his voice. "I had a test to take and everyone knows that my teachers are sticklers about missing tests. We don't get to shoot hoops at the park after school or on weekends. I overhear you arguing, and the news is talking about people getting sick. The governor said to stay home, and my friends are saying we could get sick."

Samantha Gene started crying, "I don't want to get sick."

Jose spoke up, "I guess we should have talked to you sooner. There is a virus going around called COVID-19. If we practice social distancing, wash our hooves, wear masks and stay home when we are not feeling well it will help to slow the spread of the virus.

Right now, there is a stay at home order in many states and countries. By not going to school, to work, to our family's or friend's houses, we can help to slow down the virus while the scientists and doctors are looking for some immunizations to prevent people from getting sick."

Georgia started talking, "Our job is to wash our hooves, well." She began showing the little giraffes how to wash their hooves. "Like this," she said as she showed the little giraffes proper handwashing techniques. When we go out in public we are choosing to wear face masks that grandma dropped off in our mailbox. In some areas, it is mandated to wear your mask in public.

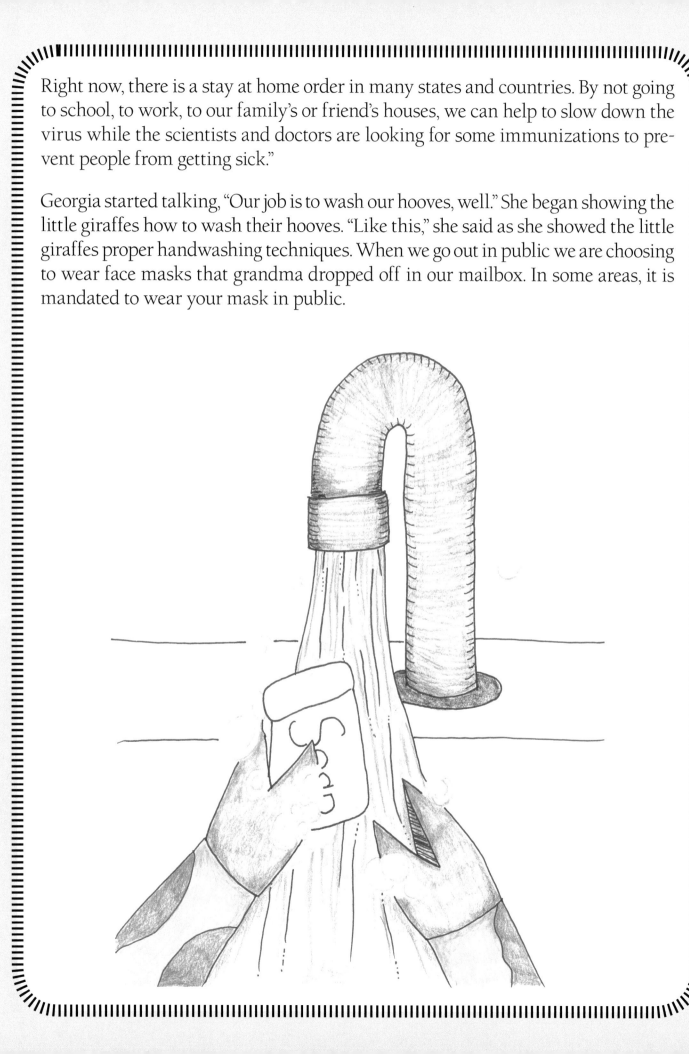

"Your teachers are figuring out a plan so that you can do your schoolwork from home and even take tests." Jersey Jack let out a groan. Georgia continued, "The doctors, nurses, and medical staff are working really hard to help everyone. They are very busy, trying to take care of people and help those that may not be feeling well because of the virus. They are also taking care of other people too because that is their job. The police are busy making sure that everyone follows the rules and is continuing to protect us. The farmers, truck drivers, and people that work at the grocery stores are making sure that we have food and everything else that we need like toilet paper to keep us safe. The mechanics are still working to make sure that our cars are running okay in case we need to go somewhere. The therapists are available to talk to you online if you feel like you want to talk to someone besides us."

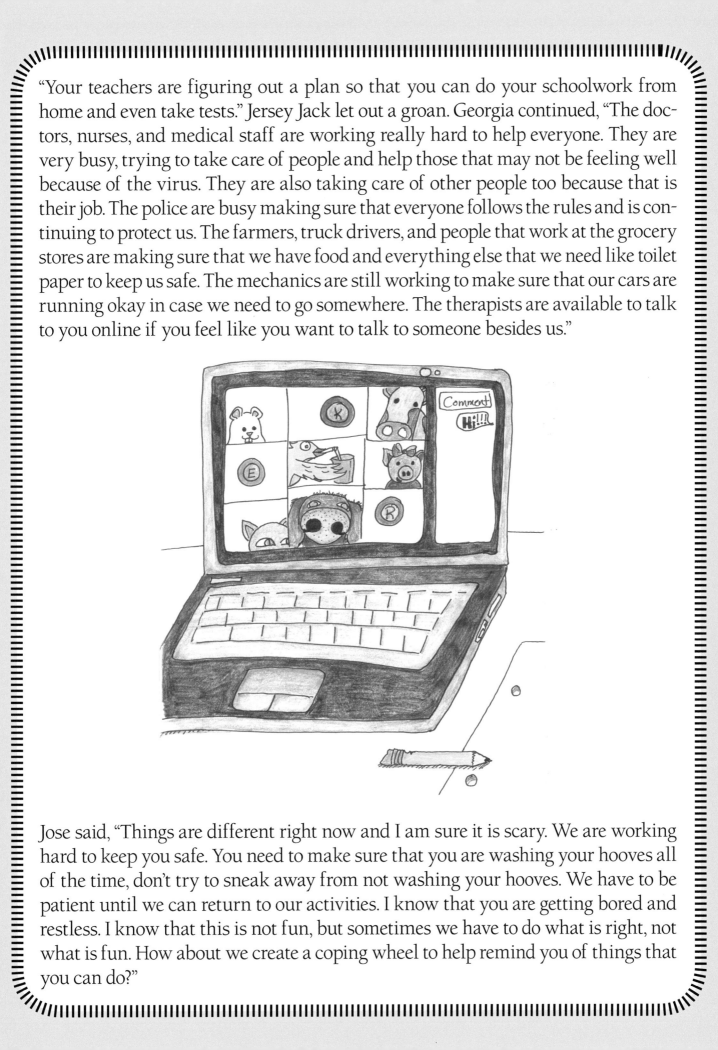

Jose said, "Things are different right now and I am sure it is scary. We are working hard to keep you safe. You need to make sure that you are washing your hooves all of the time, don't try to sneak away from not washing your hooves. We have to be patient until we can return to our activities. I know that you are getting bored and restless. I know that this is not fun, but sometimes we have to do what is right, not what is fun. How about we create a coping wheel to help remind you of things that you can do?"

Both Jersey Jack and Samantha Gene like that idea. They started rattling off a list of things that they could do. Georgia chirped up, " Whoa, let's slow down with the list. How about you each get a piece of paper, divide it like a pizza. In each one of the triangles draw and write activities that you can do to help you cope."

The little giraffes got to work.

Samantha Gene started hers. She held her hoof over it so Jersey Jack couldn't cheat off of her. In her eight triangles, she put:

1. Color
2. Sing
3. Help mama giraffe cook
4. Build Legos with Jose
5. Read a book (read along with YouTube)
6. Play with her stuffed animals
7. Go for a walk with the family
8. Watch her favorite tv show

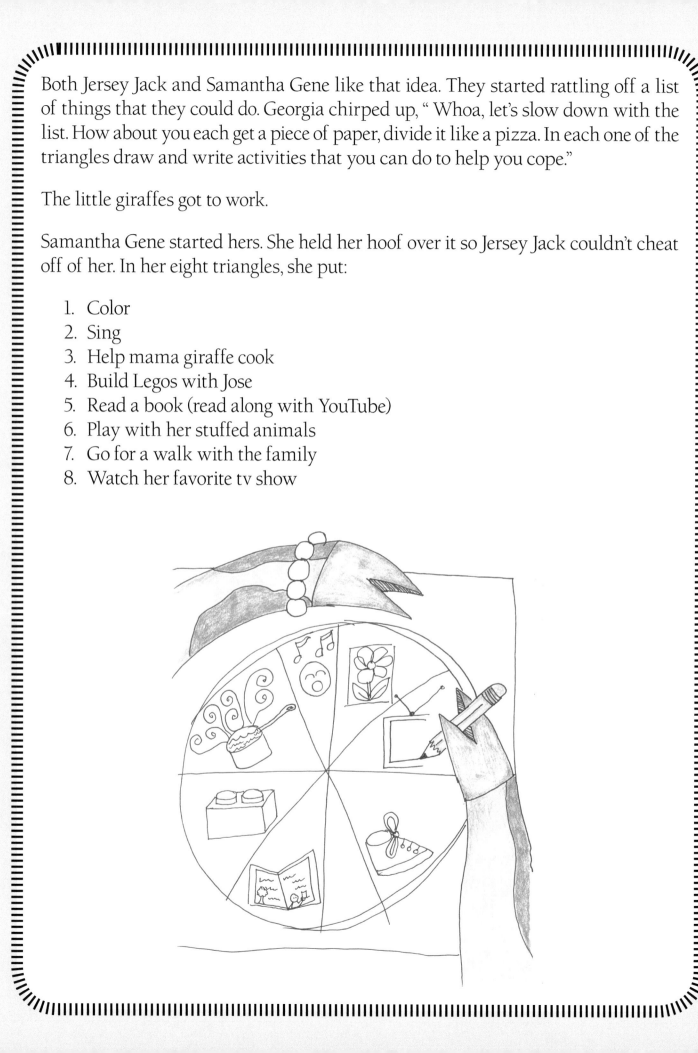

Jersey Jack's coping wheel looked a little different than Samantha's. He was more elaborate and his drawing was more precise. On his coping wheel he put:

1. Play video games with my friends
2. Ask Jose to go for a bike ride with me
3. Play board games with the family (even Chutes and Ladders with Samantha Gene)
4. Play my guitar
5. Practice baseball in the backyard. Play catch with ma or throw the ball at the target
6. Run-on the treadmill
7. Build a birdhouse with Jose
8. Play with Legos with Samantha Gene

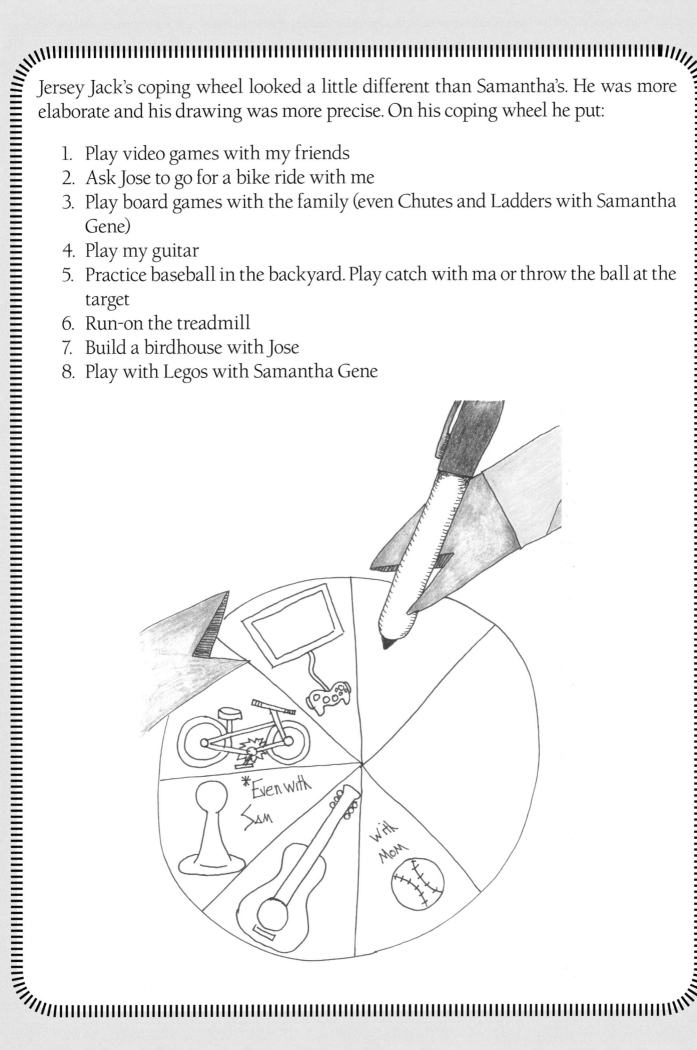

After the giraffes were done with their coping wheels, they shared, what they had written and drawn. Georgia told them that she would hang them on the refrigerator so they could see them if they were feeling sad or anxious.

Jose also taught them a grounding technique. He said, "I want you all to close your eyes."

Samantha Gene said, "Even Ma?"

"Yes, even Ma," Jose said. They all closed their eyes.

"I want you to think about your favorite place. Do not open your eyes until you can see it, smell it, hear it, and maybe feel it."

They all started envisioning their favorite places.

Samantha Gene was envisioning herself at Grandma's house.

Jersey Jack was on the baseball field. He could smell the grass and feel excitement as he was getting ready to throw out the first pitch of the game.

Georgia was at the beach with a book in her hoof, the ocean breeze blowing through her hair, and sun beaming down.

As they looked up, they all were smiling.

Jose said, "Okay, now I want you to tell me where you are this exact minute.

Georgia said, "We are in the dining room."

"Okay, name five things you can see," Jose said.

Jersey Jack said, "I see you and Ma."

Samantha Gene said, "I see the cabinet that holds the beautiful teacups."

And Georgia said, "I see the flowers that Jersey Jack picked for me out of the garden and my wonderful family!"

Jose said, "Okay. Now I want you to tell me things that you can hear This may be a little more difficult."

Samantha Gene had to strain her ears, "I hear Jersey breathing, and Jose, I hear your stomach growling."

Georgia replied, "I hear the birds chirping and the dog snoring." They all laughed.

Jersey Jack said, "I hear the clock chiming and the neighbor outside mowing."

"Now," Jose said, "Tell me five things that you can feel."

Jersey said, "I feel the table and the clothes on my back."

Georgia replied, "I feel my feet on the floor and my bangs in my eyes because I haven't been able to get a haircut."

Samantha Gene said, "I feel how tight my braids are that ma did for me this morning."

"Good," Jose said, "Now tell me five things that you can smell."

Samantha Gene said, "I smell chocolate chip cookies in the oven and the smell of ma's perfume."

Jersey Jack said, "I smell the dog's farts!" They all laughed at this.

Georgia replied, "I smell someone grilling and the fresh scent of Pinesol from all the cleaning I have been doing lately."

Jose stated, "This technique brings you to the here and now, puts a smile on your face when you think of their favorite place, and then allows you to ground yourself back to the here and now with your senses. Jose suggested practicing this technique every day so that if or when they felt worried, sad, or angry they would remember how to do it. He also told them to turn their negative thoughts into positive thoughts. Jose reminded them to make sure they are practicing building their self-esteem up by saying three good things about their character, and something good about their appearance in the mirror every day.

Georgia reminded them that their online school would begin soon. She let them know that if they ever had any questions or heard anything from their friends that caused them to worry or saddened them to know that they could always talk to them.

Jose said, "These are adult size problems, and it does cause stress on us. We love you both and we are here for you. You need to do your part by following the rules, talking to us, try not to argue, social distance, wash your hooves, get enough sleep, (but not too much), eat healthy foods and be active. We will do our part by taking care of adult size problems. If we feel that we need to update you, we will have another family meeting."

Samantha Gene piped up and said, "What is it going to look like when we can go back to school, and you can go back to work?" Georgia responded, "We don't know what normal will look like. It may look different. We may need to wear masks at school as we do at the store. The classrooms may have plexiglass dividers near your teacher's desk. Your desks may be placed 6 feet apart. You may eat lunch in your classrooms instead of the cafeteria. You may have a staggered schedule or continue with online learning. The schools are working hard with the government to determine the best way to keep us all safe. They are having meetings trying to decide how to best help students in the schools to be safe, and successful"

Jersey spoke up "What are staggered schedules? I don't like wearing a mask, are we going to have to wear a mask?"

Jose responded "Staggered schedules are where you and a small group of students may go Monday and Wednesday to school and then do some virtual learning on Tuesday and Thursdays at home while the rest of your classmates go to school. Or you may go for many hours each day. Every school district is doing what will be best for their school community. When they know what school will look like, we will too. As for the masks. Sorry, Charlie, you are just going to have to keep it on in public places until we don't have to wear them anymore"

Both Samantha Gene and Jersey Jack let out a moan, then Samantha said " I want to be able to eat lunch with all my friends in the cafeteria" Georgia replied "That might be an option but 6 feet apart. I am not sure, these are just possible scenarios that will help to keep you safe.

Jose continued to discuss with the giraffes about the changes not only in the schools but at restaurants and out in public.

He said "Don't be surprised if some businesses request that you get your temperature checked before entering the building. Also, they may ask you some questions to make sure that you are healthy and if you have a temperature you may have to go home" Things are different and change is hard but we are strong, smart, and resilient creatures. We will get through this. Some things may not ever be the same and others may go back to business as usual" Regardless of the outcome we are always here to listen to you"

Georgia looked at the two giraffes and saw that their worried faces seemed a lot more calm. She asked, "Who wants to play a board game or three?"

The little giraffes felt a lot better after talking about their feelings. They knew things weren't normal right now, but at least they understood what things they needed to do to stay safe. Georgia reminded them, "We are all in this together!"

Author Biography

 **Julie Sorenson** has been an elementary educator. She has taught as an adjunct professor at a university, teaching aspiring elementary and middle school teachers how to teach social studies. Currently, she is a School Counselor K-12 and Licensed Professional Counselor. She is in the process of completing her Doctorate of Marriage and Family Therapy. Julie is a mother of three, loves to travel, being near the water and sunsets.

Richelle Bower teaches visual arts to elementary school children and a handful of sloths in southwestern Michigan. When she isn't in the classroom, you can usually find her running on country roads or playing frisbee in the yard with her family. This is her first time illustrating a book.

Printed in the United States
By Bookmasters